The Traveling Tortellini's

P.C. Marotta

1

The Traveling Tortellini's

Written by: P.C. Marotta

pcmarotta.com

Cover Illustration by: Mary Manning

Requests for permission should be directed to:

Withers Street Press @ pcmarotta.com

withersstpress@outlook.com

ISBN-13: 978-1981299843

ISBN-10: 198129984X

For Rose

Thank You.

Table of Contents

The Trip

It was an unusually warm summer that year with just enough rainy days for grandma Pecorino's beautiful flowers to grace the village with their amazing colors. That year there were many firsts in my life, my first plane ride was one of them and oh yes, the one first I will never ever forget, that was the year we chased after the tortellini's.

The village of Scarola was a small one, if everyone didn't know you by the age of two you pretty much didn't exist at all. Rolling hills and vineyards as far as the eye could see on one side and the beautiful crystal blue sea on the other. So pretty much on one end they were making wine and on the other catching fish. I remember the stories my mother would tell me about the family gatherings when she was a little girl with all the fish you could eat, anchovies *acciughe*, mussels *cozze*, shrimp *gamberetto* and let's not forget the squid *calamaro*, which you should never get confused with Brooklyn's own Carmine Calamari, that's another story entirely to be told... but not today.

Anyways...

Mary Mozzarella lived two doors down and on any given morning, afternoon or evening you could hear her screaming for Anthony in Italian. It didn't take long to figure out what she was saying in any language!

"Anthony!.... Anthony!.... Ottenere il culo a casa i vostri padri tornare a casa!....Anthony!....Anthony!"

Which in American/Brooklynese translates to...
"Antneeee!...Antneeee!...Get your ass home, ya fartha's comin home!...Antneeeee......Antneeeee!"

All said with a Brooklyn accent of course.

By the time Friday rolled around it was Carmine Calamari who came out on the stoop and started screaming. He was praying *"Antneeeeee"* would get an apartment or change his name, we all were praying for the same thing.

The "gathering place" was centrally located in the middle of the village ...or the town ...or whatever you really want to call it but what I remember the most was my mother talking about the *"Fountain."* As tall as the eye can see... but she was a kid then so it probably wasn't very tall at all.
Every Saturday night that fountain magically turned water into wine! That's right wine...red wine... all the wine you can drink

before hitting the ground stone cold drunk! Trust me when I tell you, on the weekends there were many happy Italians dancing around that fountain. Many a night I would sit and listen to the endless stories my mother would share about her days growing up in Sicily with my grandmother. I would listen … laugh a little…but mostly they would make me smile, because I couldn't get the goofy picture out of my head of all these crazy Italians dancing in a fountain of wine!

Like I said before that year there were many firsts in my life, the plane ride was one of them. It was July fourth weekend and just like every other July fourth, my block in the Williamsburg section of Brooklyn New York was alive and kicking. It was always the four of us Frankie Fagioli, Paulie Polenta, Bobby Baccala and well yours truly... me. Together we made our way to every house in the neighborhood because we knew where the great parties, free food and the fireworks were and every fourth it was guaranteed some *"stunade"* would manage to almost blow his arms off, boy those were the good ole days. It was like a universal Italian block party, there were tables covered with food glorious food.

The Polish section had their parties going, the Irish section had their parties and we were all smart enough never to cross those boundary lines or else you would get a good ass-kicking!

Antipasto platters over flowing with provolone, salami and soppressata, fresh Italian bread still warm from Rosalie's bakery down the street, *"ugh madone"* we were overwhelmed with hunger and excitement we couldn't control ourselves...we had to eat! The songs of Julius Larosa, Vic Damone, Al Martino and Frank Sinatra filled the air in the neighborhood along with the free flowing wine and food, I don't know if we got drunk on the wine or the food or if that all was even possible! Then as if this party couldn't get any more exciting, it was as if every single person simultaneously played Lou Monte's Che La Luna Mezzo Mare and the dancing and singing began, *Ugh Madone!*

That July fourth it was not to be...

My mother and father decided we were going to see grandma Pecorino because every first Saturday of the month grandma would throw the gathering that would end all gatherings, family would come from all over and this year "yours truly" was going to be there. Sadly for me, that meant getting on a plane, I surely was going to die. I'd be away from my friends, the food, the music and the wine, the world as I knew it was coming to an end!

The adventure started the minute we stepped out the door. My father insisted on calling a cab to the airport instead of letting Bobby Baccala's father Vinny take us, that was the first mistake of the day. It was hot, the luggage was heavy and I was in no mood for any of it. As we boarded the plane I looked back one last time, I couldn't help but feel the best part of my life I was leaving behind in Brooklyn for parts unknown. We started to ascend into the blue vastness of the open skies or as my mother would say, "the closest we'll ever get to God with our eyes open." I knew right then I was surely going to die. Eight long hours and twenty five grueling minutes later, we landed in Palermo.

Grandma Pecorino… Where Are You?

Adriana Pasqualina was supposed to pick us up at the airport and take us to my grandparents house. Adriana was Capi Cannoli's *gumade* and Capi was grandpa Pecorino's friend in Scarola. Turns out… Adriana was everybody's *gumade!* In fact, legend has it *Pasta Puttanesca* was named after her, you can see where this is going.

One, two, three hours pass I have to pee so bad I was dancing the *Tarantella* at lightning speed! My mother screaming at my father so loud it became a mix of broken English-Italian slang gibberish but for some strange reason I think people around us understood it because a cab pulled up and asked us where we were going …or at least I think he did. Now keep in mind my mother was born in Sicily and my father in Brooklyn, New York and although my mother once knew Italian when she was young, it seemed she forgot all of it when she met my father so now the only real Italian they knew how to speak were broken sentences that made no sense to anybody but their Italian and Sicilian born parents and slang words so us kids wouldn't know what they were saying. Yeah right… like that worked! My father proceeded to tell the driver my grandparents address from a tiny piece of crumbled paper in the gibberish Italian-English-Brooklynese language and I could tell by the look on the driver's face, we were in a world of shit!

Believe it or not, that wasn't what worried me the most, what scared the crap out of me and everyone else was my mother screaming, *"Where's the ocean?!"* Hey, I was only along for the ride, remember this was not my idea. Finally, after what seemed to be an entire day in the back of this extremely hot non-air-conditioned cab that smelled like rotten provolone, we arrived... or did we?

My mother, father, my brother Joey, myself and two thousand pounds of luggage unload from the endless ride through the countryside. My mother kept insisting this didn't look the same as she remembered. My father insisted this was the place and yet, he really had no clue at all. At this point I was so friggin happy to get out of that car I couldn't care if we were visiting hell and Satan was the host! I have to admit, wherever we were it looked a little like Brooklyn, only more colorful. Three knocks on the door and a middle aged chubby woman about four feet six... her hair tied in a bun... apron over her house dress...stockings rolled down to her ankles and a clueless smile on her face answered the door. I swear, it was like I was in a scene from The Godfather!

"Ciao, posso aiutarti? She asked: *"*Hello, can I help you?"

"La zia Isabella, sei tu?" Aunt Isabella, is that you?

Keep in mind, my mother was reading from her Italian-English translator book...

"Ah si, si."

The Italian woman said: "Ah yes, yes."

"Sono io, Sophia da Brooklyn a New York!"

My mother once again explained: "It's me, Sophia from Brooklyn New York!"

"Ah...si si, l'America!" Isabella exclaimed: "Ah...yes, yes, America!"

As the door opened wider, strange faces I've never seen before in pictures or heard about all smiling and nodding, about what... I had no idea. Hand gestures motioning us at lightning speed to come in and sit down, I was getting dizzy. Okay, I thought... I can handle this and anyhow the food smelled incredible so for what it was worth, I was going to eat! While the language barrier was getting more and more horrific, the food was an Italian kid from Brooklyn's dream come true.

First the fresh baked crusty bread came out of the warm brick oven. Then family members started bringing in the platters of prosciutto, soppressata di calabria, green olives, grilled eggplant, I thought I died and was in Italian heaven! I was so high from the aromas of the Italian feast before me I completely forgot about the intense language barrier between my parents and these generous folks feeding my "*gavone*" appetite. Just then… I hear my mother say or try to say to this woman they've been calling Aunt Isabella.

"*Dove si trova mama Pecorino?*" my mother asked.

"Where is mama Pecorino?"

"*Pecorino?*" said the old woman.

"*Ah si, si uno minuti!*"

"Ah yes, yes one minute!"

I had no idea where she disappeared to, maybe she was going to get grandma she looked very happy nodding her head and smiling again with a lot of hand gestures…always the hand gestures! She reminded me of Bobby Baccala's crazy grandmother from Sicily who liked to pinch your cheeks till they bled.

All of a sudden "Aunt Isabella" comes back with the biggest tray of Italian cheeses I'd ever seen! They must have a cheese factory somewhere in the house! Provolone, Caciocavallo, Incanestrato, Mozzarella, Provolo, Ricotta, Scamorza and PECORINO!

"*NO! NO!*" my mother said in a voice that was now at least five octaves higher than before. Now my father, who was thoroughly enjoying the feast before him, stuffing his face like it was the last supper…was nodding in agreement like he had a clue what was being said in the mass confusion taking place around him until my mother's hand met the back of his head—*Smaaack!*…and then she said it…

"Antneeeeeeeeeee!, Oh my gawd who are these friggin' people?" said my mother who calmly whispered into my father's ear while her brain was on fire!

"And where's grandma Pecorino?"

"And why are you just sitt'n there stuff'n your face!?"

She looked at them…they looked at her…still smiling and nodding and of course no one knew exactly what each one was saying. I felt the panic in the air like being struck by lightning it was something to write home about. All of a sudden, my mother gets up calmly and what seemed to be in slow motion and all a blur turns to the Italian family, smiling and says…

"E' cosi bella in questo periodo dell'anno in Scarola."

"It's so beautiful this time of year in Scarola."

Just then it was the land of confusion eight Italian faces looked around at each other like they had just landed on the moon and had no idea how they got there. The woman my mother thought was "Aunt Isabella" stepped forward and said…

"No questo e Scattola, non Scarola. scarola e in questo modo!"

"No, no this is Scattola, not Scarola. Scarola is that way!"

Let me get this straight...

Wrong family...wrong village...wrong aunt and we have no idea where "that way" leads!

Scarola!

Peppino Porchetta lived a stones throw away from our new found Aunt Isabella and her generous family. When he heard of our misfortune as did the entire town by now, he offered to take us to Scarola. I'm guessing the trip we were about to embark on to Scarola will not be a quick one... as usual my father's Brooklynese/Italian just wasn't cutting it with the locals but yet he persisted with crumbled and now torn map in hand asking how far the trip will be. Peppino must have gotten some idea of what my father was trying to convey as he watched my father wildly banging his hand on the map and pointing to who knows where and Peppino nodding in agreement with lot's of hand gestures pointing down the road... a very long road. I knew we were getting close to Scarola because my mother not only scared the shit out of Mr. Porchetta, my father and my brother Joey, she woke up everyone who was and wasn't dead yet in Italy with her screams...

"I see the ocean!... Antneeeee look it's the friggin ocean!"

"Holy Crap Sophia!", my father shouted.

I'm not ready to go friggin deaf yet, calm down!"

All I smelled was fish, dead, gross, foul smelling fish, which reminded me of the summers going out to Jones Beach driving the Jones Beach Causeway with my father on one of his many fishing weekends, it also reminded me of Adriana Pasqualina for some strange reason—that too, is another story.

Anyways...

By now, the one hundredth hour had descended upon us and my brother Joey had to pee and yours truly was dying of thirst. I thought, *"dear God, let me die now"* and just as I opened my eyes... Scarola! There it was... *The Fountain!* The majestic, stone cold drunk, wine flowing friggin fountain and how majestic it was! Just a few houses down the road and we really did arrive. While Peppino Porchetta helped my father unload the luggage all four thousand pounds of it, I watched my brother Joey try anxiously to open the car door as if I was watching a man on fire running toward a hose.

Once again I rolled my eyes and told him to *"Watch Out!"* while I kicked the door with my foot...easier said than done. The door flies open and my brother follows, down to the ground he goes on all fours. I tried not to laugh but after all we've been through getting here I thought... what the hell. Watching him brush himself off I noticed something smelled really bad...

"Holy shit, Joey, you stink!" I said proudly and nauseated at the same time.

"What?" he said. Totally unaware of what was going on which you would expect from an eleven year old.

"I'm tell'n Ma!"

Wouldn't ya know it, my brother peed himself right there in the car. He probably was part of that foul fish smell.

Anyways...

Scarola, the beautiful village of vineyards and fish. The sky was the bluest I've ever seen and there was a gentle breeze in the air, it was all so picture perfect. *Naaa...* who am I kidding... we all looked like hell, disheveled and in disarray badly in need of showers and clean clothes especially my brother who now smelled like an outhouse... but here we were, finally at grandma Pecorino's house in Sicily.

"Sophiaaaaaa!" Grandma cried out.

"Finalmente fatta qui, guarda tutti voi." "You finally made it here, look at all of you!"

"Ognuno sembra meraviglioso!" she said. "Everyone looks wonderful!"

I'm assuming grandma must have vision problems because wonderful would not have been my first choice of words to describe us. Grandma looked just as she did in all the photo's I had seen of her, short and round with beautiful skin and sparkling eyes behind her gold rimmed glasses and her salt and pepper hair tied neatly in a bun. When she grabbed me and hugged me she smelled so good—clean like freshly washed clothes hanging on an outside line on a spring day. For that moment I felt like I've known this woman for years, like I've seen her everyday when in fact, this was the first time I've met her in person. Her hug seemed to take the drama of this trip from hell and melt it all away, it was all going to be okay from here on in...*Yea, right.*

Grandpa Pecorino was as tall as grandma, not much bigger than five-foot-four, maybe. With a thick head of white hair and mustache to match brought out his sky blue eyes. I have to admit, both my grandparents were pretty good looking and must have been real 'knock outs' in their younger days. I can seriously see where my mother gets her good looks and loud mouth from. Scarola reminded me so much of Brooklyn, without the accent. Grandma and grandpa lived in a really ginormous house with an upstairs and over-looking the ocean! In the village, all the street lined homes were close together like soldiers standing shoulder to shoulder. The streets were cobblestone and not wide at all. Everyone drove just like in New York, crazy and always in a hurry but in very small cars, mopeds and bicycles and everything was colorful even the stone streets! When the sun hit the buildings they almost looked pink, peach and blue. Everything popped with color and flowers everywhere. I felt like I was in a painting, like in a dream. I must have been delirious and dehydrated from the long trip...that's it. Every window had planters filled with beautiful flowers and colored plants with vines that reached the ground below.

Inside grandma's house was an entirely different world from the apartments we have in Brooklyn, it was huge. In Brooklyn if your scratching your ass in the bedroom your friends can see you from the kitchen. We had what they called *'railroad rooms'* and if your mother's running after you with a broom your only escape is out the window onto the fire-escape or under the bed...not very many choices there. In grandma's house the first floor was wide open with so many windows that you can see the sand and water in the distance and in the kitchen a real brick oven! All I could think of was pizza and telling the guys back home of this wonderful different world.

The walls in grandma's house were covered in framed photos of family that seemed to be taken a million years ago, so many people wearing black—black dresses, black shoes, black hats. I knew the photo's were in black and white with shades of gray but they were all wearing black! Nonetheless they were family and people who I will never meet because well.....they're dead.

Back in the kitchen, grandma was serving espresso coffee and the Anisette was flowing freely. My parents were laughing and grandpa was telling a family story or two and for some strange reason Peppino Porchetta was still there. My brother had changed into clean clothes and didn't smell anymore but wait a few hours that will eventually change, it always does.

At that moment I decided to break free and explore outside before the weekend festivities begin and the entire family descends on Scarola.

The Family

I couldn't wait to tell Bobby Baccala back in Brooklyn that they were wrong about Italy. My friends would always say, *"There's no Italians like Brooklyn Italians,"* come to find out all Italians originated in Italy first. How *stunade* could we all be? Apparently...very! Then again, this was Bobby Baccala the original smart-ass of Williamsburg and even when wrong... was always right.

Anyways...

It was my duty to report home to everyone so I took pictures and boy did I take pictures! I promised myself I would be a world traveler and take pictures of everything, you know, so I had proof when asked important questions like *"what did the bathrooms look like"* and *"what time was dinner served"* all that important stuff. I needed to look educated and worldly.

Okay... back to reality here.

I finally arrived at the *"Fountain"* you know the majestic miraculous fountain that makes everybody drunk on Saturday night but today was different than most days, people were hustling to and fro like a colony of well trained ants on a mission. I looked down at myself, waiting to see what would happen if I suddenly moved, it seemed, everyone was moving in warped speed and I was in slow motion. I looked up, the sun was out and not a cloud in the deep blue sky, the bluest I'd ever seen. I could see the sea in the distance a beautiful color of turquoise like Frankie's mother's ring that is too big for her fingers. I could see in the distance men in white hats putting up tents. No, not the cheap camping tents we used to buy that our father's swore would never leak or blow down with a strong wind, not that kind. These were big huge white tents with long metal legs the kind you could fit a ton of people under like in a concert or big block party! That's what we needed in Brooklyn next year, I have to make a note of this... I'll take pictures.

It seemed every year my dad took all of us upstate camping near the Mohonk Preserve hiking in the heat and the mosquitoes as big as B-52 bombers were my favorite part of the trip...said no one ever! We would all settle into our campsite and build a fire and my dad would tell us camping stories which usually wound up to be horror stories with the sounds of strange animals in the background for special effects. What I remember the most were the tents and the many nights it rained...no it didn't just rain...the skies opened up with a vengeance and our little campsite was always the target. A big bulls-eye right on us for ole-mother-nature herself. The water proof tents were not so water proof anymore. Maybe a big huge tent with metal legs over us would have been just what we needed to keep us dry from mother nature's fury but I couldn't figure out why the white hats. Were they having a sale on white hats? Maybe it was proper tent attire here or a fashion statement...who knows?

Meanwhile... I could hear women laughing and chattering about what? I hadn't a clue. They were carrying tablecloths, white tablecloths to match the white tents not the vinyl kind we have at home with the felt backing, no these were real cloth with napkins to match. The kind my mother would put out for holidays only and God-forbid you dropped any gravy on them! I never understood that they were there to wipe your mouth and you couldn't get them dirty. Go figure! The people kept coming with gifts, with wine, with luggage you name it... they had it.

They brought their dogs too! They came in fancy cars, and limos! Yes, limo's!...Holy crap! Some even arrived by the type of plane that lands on the water! Okay, now I'm really dreaming and I'm in the movie *The Godfather* and waiting for Martin Scorsese to yell, *"aaaand ACTION!"* No one would believe this especially Bobby's friend around the corner Bambi Boombats who thought she was all that because her father owned a six family next to Rafaello Risotto's funeral parlor, big fuckin deal so they live near dead people how fuckin exciting ...I bet weekends are really hopping there!

Speaking of hopping, here comes the band!

Holy crap...a ten piece band on a band stage set up right by the sea! *"Who throws parties like this!?"* I found myself saying out loud. Just then, I hear *"pssssst...pssssst...."* and poke on the shoulder. *"What!"* I yelled.

"You hungry?" A woman's voice whispered.

"You speak English!" I said in a shocking, harmonious yell. *"Si, Si."*

Oh no, here we go again with the Italian, I'm screwed now.

I followed her anyway I figured what the hell, I was tired of watching people in white set up tents... in white for the world's largest party with no color coordination whatsoever!

She led me just a few doors down in the opposite direction from the party site past a few of the pretty colored houses and there it was, right in front of me I hit it rich! Fast food on wheels Italian style! A cart with all you can eat...fresh fruit, pastries, cheeses and meats. I had to take pictures while I was stuffing my face at lightning speed.

"Eat, eat!" she said, pointing to all the food!

"Holy crap!" I thought, all they do is eat in this part of the world.

This was turning out to be a pretty good day.

Meanwhile, back at grandma's house the festivities were off and running. People were coming and going, kissing and smiling and shaking hands. Apparently, we have a lot of family members I didn't know about and never heard about...and trust me when I tell you, they were quite the bunch. There were the "S" cousins Sal Sfogliatelle, Santino Struffoli, Savino Stugatz, Sergio Stunade and Stefano Sfacime who all wore black suits, black hats, black shirts with...you guessed it...black ties. I guess they forgot to tell them the funeral was over... and they all dated Susanna Spostata who was with them wearing what the old women were saying was a handkerchief around her ass as a dress. Her hair was jet black and shiny with pearly white skin and blood red lips. She reminded me of Snow White without the cute costume and I guess Snow White never wore 9-inch heels either. I watched through the window as they approached grandma's house and kissed her hand one by one. They all looked like wise guys disciplined by a little old lady with a bun and an apron. At that moment I wasn't sure if I should take pictures of this for fear they may break or eat my camera. I just made a mental note of all this for future reference... like when I'm in the witness protection program!

There was cousin after cousin walking on what appeared to be a cement runway to grandma's house. There was Regina Romano who came with her caravan of luggage like she was moving to Sicily permanently. I swear there had to be a body in that trunk! Piece after piece of luggage one bigger than the other all carried by these men dressed in chauffeur uniforms with hats. Either she was rich or as we would say in Brooklyn, *"Doin Them All."* She wore this floral dress hiked way up high with what looked like 30 inch heels, spiky heels at that and this big wide brimmed fancy hat on her head with her long black wavy hair softly blowing in the breeze as she sashayed up the endless runway to grandma's.

Then there was Gabby Gabbadost and cousin Dino Disgraziat they were "best friends" so they say. He was about five feet two and one hundred and twenty pounds soaking wet and she was three hundred pounds give or take a few. Rumor has it, they were an item. When I saw them walking down the endless walkway or as I called it, *"the runway to grandma's house"* I felt like I wanted to run into a wall a few times to get the image of the both of them *"doin it"* out of my mind! The poor guy was carrying a few hundred pounds of luggage while she was telling him something in a very loud squeaky ear-piercing voice eating what looked like an entire loaf of Italian bread. I guess she wanted to get started on the food early.

Paulina Pesce and Isabella Frittata weren't cousins they were considered family anyway...you know, gumades. They were grandma's oldest friends. You could tell they were friends with grandma because they all looked like they wore the same house dresses. Lot's of flowers, snaps down the middle and short sleeves. Salt and pepper hair rolled in the back in neatly placed buns and black shoes with a little heel and black purses to match. *Match? ...Nothing matched!*

But hey, who am I ... surely not the fashion police!

It took them forever to get close to grandma's house from the "runway" and of course had to pinch my cheeks like they were taking skin samples back to the lab for analyzing! But all in all they meant well. It took an entire month for the redness to leave my face but that's another story.

Benny Biscotti and Paulie Parmigiana were Carlotta Puttana's sons...don't ask. You pretty much can figure this one out all on your own. Benny and Paulie are considered what you would call, "mama's boys". They were in their fifities and still unmarried and living with mom. They looked like gangsters to me... but hey who am I? Once again, black suits with black shirts and this time...white ties. Their heads were donned with black hats with a white sash around them, a red handkerchief in their jacket pocket and last but not least, spectator shoes. Give me a break...I'm a kid but I notice these things! They had big gold rings on their pinky fingers and watches that glistened in the sun. In front of them was their mom, Carlotta Puttana. I heard she was in her seventies but she didn't look a day over forty if that was at all possible. She looked like a movie star, like Myrna Loy or Betty Grable. She too was dressed in black! What's with all the black I thought, holy crap! It's like a funeral party instead of a regular party maybe somebody did die and I didn't know it. No, it couldn't be I would have heard all the ladies crying and carrying on.

Anyways...

She was dressed in black. Black skirt suit with a black hat and beautiful white blond hair short and wavy under the big brimmed hat. Around her shoulders she wore a dead animal! It was a fox like thing all furry with a head and feet and tail! I sometimes would see fancy ladies in Brooklyn wear these things around their necks. I used to pull my mother's out of the closet when she wasn't looking and pretend they were my very own dogs to play with ...*shhhh...* she still doesn't know. I wonder if Bennie and Paulie killed it for her... they probably did but you didn't hear that from me.

I had no idea we had this many family members! They just kept coming...and coming...and coming! I heard some of them come to grandma's party every year! Who the hell has that kind of money? Every year? Are you fuckin kidding me!? It was like a carnival everyone was dressed to the nines all like in costumes or their Sunday best. In Brooklyn we only wear our good clothes when it's a holiday, Sunday mass or when someone dies. These people looked like they have nothing but good clothes, they probably go to a lot of funerals!

Thank God most of them don't know who I am yet, they haven't noticed me over where I was standing except for grandma's old lady friends, I can still feel the blood pooling in my cheeks. Everyone kissing and hugging like they see each-other every day! How come I was never informed of these so called "family" members! After this trip is over, I have to have a sit down with my parents and discuss family because I just know there's important information that's probably on a need-to-know basis and I need to know!

Just as I heard the words, *"Holy Crap!"* come flying out of my mouth I see this huge stretch limo pull up all the way down the "runway" as far as the eye can see. I had to get a good view for this one. I looked down to see what I can stand on. A concrete pot with a plant in it will do just fine, so I dump the plant, turn over the pot and I have some leverage to view the show.

No...wait...not one limo but two!

Two big stretch limos. This had to be good, this was worth taking pictures because everyone back home would never believe this. There were eight guys and four ladies and you guessed it....*all in black!*

There was Frankie Bracciole, Charlie Cioppino, Robbie Ravioli and Sammy Sirloin. They all looked tough but not as tough as the next four! Nicky No Thumbs, Izzy The Iceman, Freddie The Fish and Sonny The Sausage all had beautiful ladies with them. Trust me, these guys were not runners up for GQ Magazine.

Everyone just stopped and smiled as they walked by. Were they here to kill someone? Maybe it is a funeral party and they didn't kill the person yet! *Holy crap!* I couldn't stand it anymore I had to go inside grandma's house to see what everyone was doing. My parent's had to be there, it was safe there. I just kept telling myself that and I had to believe it. If that didn't work...there were plenty of beds to hide under.

Meanwhile people were milling about all over grandma's house. It was packed with family and friends all talking Italian and English and some a little of both. I needed a drink maybe if I could sneak some wine and pass out I'll wake up back in Brooklyn and this all would have been a very funny dream. Just then someone pokes me on the back. I thought I'd been made...I was caught! I felt the blood rush from my head and my legs got heavy and my brow was wet with sweat and just then I hear...

"Hey, where were ya?"

It was my brother Joey standing their with sauce on his face eating pepperoni bread.

"Ahhhhhhh!.... Don't ever scare the shit out of me again like that!" I screamed.

"Hey! Hey!... what's going on here?"

My father interrupted as I was about to choke my brother.

"Eat something then get cleaned up, the party's going to start in a couple of hours."

" You're lucky!" I said pointing my finger in my brother's face as I turned to get something to eat, I was starving!

Everyone was coming around to taste grandma's famous tortellini salad, I kid you not! The three cheese tortellini handmade from scratch, artichoke hearts from artichokes home grown, roasted peppers from, what else, home grown peppers roasted on the fire, olives meticulously picked from grandpa himself and the list goes on. The dressing from all natural home grown ingredients and apparently my grandmother was famous throughout the entire village for her salad, which I thought was weird but hey, this entire trip was weird. The bowls she spooned the salad in were huge who could possibly carry one of these bowls! Maybe they call the Italian army to bring the tanks to haul the bowls! The streets are too narrow, that wouldn't work. Come to find out before these huge monster bowls make their entrance to the feast, there's a "test bowl" oh yes, my grandmother and grandfather have to test the salad and approve of it before it makes it's grand entrance. *"In what other world does this happen... and where am I?* Give me a fork, spoon or I could use my hands or stick my entire friggin face in the bowl it had to be good...this was Sicily! By the way...the kitchen smelled amazing!

Everyone got little matching bowls that matched the big "test" bowl all waiting for grandma to carefully spoon tortellini salad into their bowl. Like salivating puppies at dinner time everyone lined up waiting patiently. As I turned my head I got the shock of my life, the line to "test" grandma's salad was so long I couldn't see the end of it. It looked like they were lined up to ask the Don for favors!   Then it was my turn, patiently waiting spoonful by spoonful and there it was, my bowl filled with grandma's salad and it smelled so good. This was the moment and the anticipation was killing me. I slowly lifted the spoon filled with tortellini, roasted peppers an olive or two and feta cheese to my watering mouth, passed the lips and onto my tongue and then it happened...

The sun was shining...the angels singing...the wind blowing gently through my hair and the birds gathering around to greet me...oh no, their gathering because I'm dropping food and how did I get outside? That's funny I can hear the angels singing and it's getting louder and louder, could it be that grandma's tortellini salad transports you to heaven?

Wait, those are no angels...it's grandma screaming!

The Tortellini's

I can't quite explain the events that followed on that day. Even now, many years later it all seems a blur. Like the time Giuseppe Pignoli got hit in the face with a baseball, Vinny Vafungool didn't mean to pitch that ball so fast, but in the blink of an eye he was down, and now that I look back I think that's why he repeats every word twice.

The screaming and crying got louder and louder. The women were running around wailing with their hands in the air, and the men were all huddled in various groups talking and pointing fingers at what, no one knew. There were so many people screaming in Italian it sounded like one big siren going off in my head. I wanted to move, but I was frozen in place with a fork in one hand and the little 'test' bowl in the other. I didn't know whether to run away or continue eating this amazing salad...I ate the salad. Grandma's salad was so delicious and amazing that I hardly noticed the intense chaos happening all around me. Just then, I feel someone tugging on my shirt only to notice it was my brother Joey.

"What do you want!" I said, wanting to stick the fork in his hand.

"Look!...Look!...Over there, hurry!" he said, with eyes as big as

the 'test' bowl itself. Just then I turned around as if it were in the slowest motion possible, like the earth was slowing it's rotation, and there it was I couldn't believe my eyes. The group of guys that included Freddie The Fish and Izzie The Iceman also included this tremendously gigantic guy who they called Tomaso Bolognese, he had to be nine feet tall! All speaking in what I would assume to be Italian, but who knows maybe they had their own code language like Bobby Baccala and I when we don't want our parents to know what we're saying. Well, this giant of a guy starts to pull out what I swear was a gun! *Yes...a gun!*

I felt the blood rush from my brain and I thought I swallowed my tongue as my eyes tried to jump out from their sockets. Then I heard it, the sound that stopped Italy in it's tracks, you know like the shot heard round the world...yep, that's it. *CRRRRASH!* From my hands to the stone floor below, the one...the only...TEST BOWL! Standing there mouth open, heart stopping and brain freezing, I noticed everyone was silent and looking in my direction. This was bad...very...very bad. At that very moment my very short life passed before my eyes, and all I could see were these scary ass goons in black staring in my friggin direction, and moving toward me. That's when my brother Joey, who I thought for sure was halfway home by now, screamed the most beautiful word in the world..."*RUUUUUUN!*"

I never realized how fast a human being can run when they fear for their life, let me tell you, it's pretty damn fast. I kept thinking this was it, I was gonna die the way '*Rats*' die and not the kind that are furry and squeak either. They were gonna fit me with cement shoes, I looked down at my lightening fast feet..."*Oh God, they're gonna be pretty small!,*" or they'll chop me up and I'll be placed all around Italy....no, wait...New York...that's it, I'll be shipped out like frozen meat. Just then I heard myself scream as we were running through grandma's ginormous house.

"*Oh God...Joey...Ruuuuuuuuun!*"

We made it, I don't know how, but we made it...out the door and the light of day shined upon us. Still in panic mode and ready to flee the scene of crime of the broken bowl, we stopped for a moment and looked around.

"*Look!*" said my brother Joey, as he pointed to a billion people in their own panic mode. *"The big scary men must be after them too!"*

"C'mon," I said. As I grabbed his hand and we started to survey just what the hell was going on.

It was insane chaos! Sicilians running in every direction yelling and waving their hands in the air. I swear I saw one lady run over to the *Fountain* like she was going to throw herself into the giant pool of wine, but instead, she was cupping her hands and drinking the wine like it was the last drink she would ever have, all the while yelling or praying or swearing in Italian, Sicilian and every other language it seemed and it wasn't just her doing it.

Joey and I just stood still by the *Fountain* while we watched in total confusion. If any family member at this point was looking for us, which I know they weren't, they would have never found us. We stood....we watched....there were short Italian men standing around in groups, they wore hats like our newspaper boy back home...they were whispering and looking around and pointing fingers in all directions. There were women, lots of women in house dresses with aprons and buns in their hair, screaming and waving their hands in the air, some were beating their chests like they do in church and looking to the sky...I have to admit...that was scary. One lady who was much younger with long hair was moving her head wildly in a circular motion and her eyes looked like they were gonna disappear in her head, just then I felt my brother tug at my shirt.

"What is it, Joey?" I said annoyingly.

" God's coming."

"I think you're right this time Joey. For once in your life, I think you're right."

We stood perfectly still, we looked around...

He tugged at my shirt again.

"What now, Joey!"

"Is God really coming?" Joey asked again.

"I don't know Joey, I don't know anything at this point. If God is fuckin coming Joey, then you'll have a hell of show to tell at school."

The five minutes that went by felt like five friggin hours and either the sun was hot or I was about to pop a vein or something, and there goes the tug on my shirt again....

"WHAT!" I screamed so loud it sounded like a whisper over all the noise.

"Is God coming?"

Now, keep in mind my brother knew he was annoying me to death even in the middle of a strange village that was erupting like Pompeii. He just always had to be a pain in the ass!

"YES JOEY, GOD IS FUCKIN COMING AND YOU'RE GOING BACK WITH HIM!"

Okay, now I think three people standing next to us where the only ones that weren't screaming or wailing and the were close enough to hear me because they both turned around to look at me with a really nasty look on their faces. I gave them my 'don't bother me' Brooklyn look and middle finger, I think it worked.

At this point it was getting hot, I was getting a bit nervous not knowing what really was happening and my brother was becoming a hemorrhoid. I took my brother's hand and we started to walk our way through the madness past grandma's house where the screaming and wailing was really loud and it seemed most of the people were running in and out of her front door. Just then, I see my mom…

"MAAAAAAAAA!" I yell at the top of my lungs.

"Oh my gawd…where have you both been, I've been worried sick!"

"What the hell is goin on here?"

"Oh my gawd, it's grandma, that's what happened."

"GRANDMA!?…did she….?"

"Oh my gaaaawd….NO! It's the salad…someone stole the real tortellini salad and the entire village is going crazy!"

By now I seriously thought I took a stroke and I wasn't understanding my mother, I mean ….I heard the words come out of her mouth but I couldn't understand them, or perhaps I was in a coma and this was a really bad nightmare.

Either way….what the fuck was she talk'n about here!

I heard myself scream….

"What the fuck are you talk'n about, ma?!"

Just then I felt her five fingers sweep across my burning red cheeks.....*SMAAAAAACK!*

"What the hell was that for?... Has everyone here lost their mind?...what the hell?

Now my mother looked like she was in the CIA. She was acting nervous, her eyes darting from side to side making sure no one was listening or maybe making sure those crazy family members in black didn't find her....what the hell was I thinking? No one can find her, she couldn't find me, we couldn't find her...the entire friggin village can't find a god-damn salad! I really need to get back to Brooklyn.

She continued to say...

" No...No...shhhhh...they're all looking for it."

"Looking for what........MAAAAAAAA?" I said very slowly so she would understand every letter in every word.

" The salad, you don't understand...it's the salad."

Shaking my head in disbelief I started to turn away, still holding on to my brother's hand, just then it happened...the tug on my shirt.

"What Joey, I'm in no mood right now!"

"I have to pee."

Sure enough there he was holding his 'winky' jumping up and down looking up at me.

Will someone please remind me why I agreed to come on this fuckin trip...

Hostage

While standing on a corner holding up a wall waiting for my brother to finish his "business" I thought to myself...*how does an entire town lose their minds over a salad?* Two years ago my brother got lost in the mall in Queens and no one noticed he was missing until we were all back in the car ready to go home. And what about those guys in black? What about those guys in black that are family? And what's with grandma? Grandmothers are supposed to be sweet and frail and bake things and cook things that we all love. Bobby Baccala's grandmother, Mrs. Sfacime is always in the kitchen singing and stirring something in a big pot. How do I explain my grandmother in Sicily is secretly part of the Mafia...although this too can work in my favor...

Just then I realized my brother either has the bladder of a 90-year-old man or something is very wrong. As I push my way through all the screaming Italians running frantically through the streets to the little grassy area between the buildings where Joey said he was going to pee, I noticed he wasn't there.

My heart began to race, I could feel my face become flush with sweat pouring down my cheeks. I imagined that I could feel my hair turn gray, if that's possible. I was a kid and this can't be happening to me I thought. I looked right, I looked left, I swiftly turned around and looked towards the **Fountain**...the wine stopped flowing and no Joey. I was standing at the corner of "I want to go home" and "what should I be buried in" and the sun was hot or that was just my blood boiling. A woman frantically ran up to me and grabbed my shoulders and screamed in Italian...

Dov'e l'insalataaaaaa!! "Where's the salaaaaad!"

Just as fast as she screamed those words was as fast as she ran away into the mad panicked screaming crowd. It actually reminded me of the Godzilla movies that I would watch on Saturday mornings, you know where all the people would run wildly through the streets to get away from Godzilla...yeah, that's exactly how it looked. I started screaming for my brother, *Joeeeey!...Joeeeey!...Joeeeeeey!*...then I heard it...

I'm heeeere...I'm heeeere!

Oh thank goodness, there he was sitting in the doorway of a plane. A PLANE!... What the hell was he doing in a plane and more importantly, why was this plane (a small one mind you) parked on the beach where the party was going to be...or is going to be...I'm so confused. I started to run towards my brother whose now sitting with his feet dangling happily out of the doorway of a small private plane like it's an amusement ride which is parked facing the ocean on the beach where this Italian/Sicilian party of unknown family and friends was supposed to take place, in a town where every person is running around like the village-loons looking for a tortellini salad that my grandmother who I never met before made in a country I've never been to before, until now. Sounds pretty normal to me, I wonder if this can get a write up in the Daily News back home...nah nobody died...not yet anyway.

As I'm running toward Joey I look to my right and in the distance I saw them, the so called "family members" all in black and all walking towards...you guessed it...THE PLANE! There was Nickie No Thumbs, Izzie The Iceman, Freddie The Fish and Sonny The Sausage, they were the scariest bunch of family I've ever seen, all in black with black hats to match.

I finally made it to the plane in a wild panic and out of breath when my brother started to say...

" I found the salad for grandma!"

"Joey, we have to get off this plane...NOW!"

Sure enough there was the salad, packed in ice in a crate on a plane going to who knows where.

"Joey, listen to me carefully...WE HAVE TO GET OFF THIS PLANE ...NOW!"

"No, we have to take the salad back to grandma!"

At this point I was losing my patience and we were both running out of time.

"Okay," I said. *"We'll take the salad, you take one end and I'll take the other but we have to hurry."*

Let me say this…some ideas sound better when they're just ideas. The crate with the bowl and the ice were dead weight. I pulled, he pushed and pushed too hard and I fell back almost falling out of the plane's door. With my head now hanging out of the door opening I turn to see those scary so called "family members" walking up to the tail of the plane and my guess was that they weren't showing each other how pretty the shiny new plane was, my guess was we were all going for a ride…and I was right.

I got up as fast as lightning, faced my brother and said, *"HIDE!"*

"What's wrong?"

"Joey, remember that plane ride we took to get here?"

"Yea."

"Well, we're going on another one, so shut up and hide!"

As I covered his mouth with one hand I pushed him under the same canvas tarp that the salad crate was under with the other, then I covered both of us and prayed.

It had to be four hundred degrees under that tarp, breathing hard and sweating profusely I was listening for those tall scary goons to board the plane, it was eerily silent so I dared to peek. I motioned to my brother to keep quiet, as quiet as can be and to stay down…no matter what happens…stay down! I lift the tarp just a bit to let some light in and to see what I can see without being seen, and I have to admit the plane was pretty fancy…you know one of those private ones that musicians and celebrities take all over the world and in this case…people that want to kill you.

No one was on the plane yet and in my insane imagination I thought we could make a run for it, that was until I saw them…it was Nickie No Thumbs, Izzie The Iceman, Freddie The Fish and Sonny The Sausage…you know, your average family members that show up with a Bundt cake, wine and guns at holiday gatherings. They had to be waiting for someone to join them, maybe the pilot…maybe my grandmother because at this point anything was up for grabs. Then I saw him, walking tall and sturdy with all the confidence of a killer, a real ladies man the wine you and dine you type, you know the kind that buys you diamonds and a coffin at the same time…that kind of good looking. It was Sammy Sirloin…yes another *family member!* They all greeted each other and then it happened, he put on a pilot's cap…*Who the hell put's on a pilot's cap in an all black suit?! Does he even know how to fly or is this learn as you go time?* They started walking towards the plane, I made a b-line under the tarp and started to pray…. and boy did I pray. I must have said prayers I never learned in languages I've never heard!

They closed the door to the plane and started to converse with each other surprisingly in English and not Italian which was very good for me especially in the situation my brother and I were in at the moment...

"Hey Nick, you got the salad?"

"Yeah Iz, you want me to go check? It's in the back in the crate."

"Yeah, that's a good idea...go check make sure it's there and that nobody left it at the fuckin house."

Okay... now as if my life couldn't get any worse...it just did. I motioned to my brother Joey who by now was probably suffering from heat exhaustion to continue to be quiet at all costs which now meant certain death. I thought of my mom and dad who by now were probably sick with worry looking for us...*nah who am I kidd'n*...she's probably on her ninth glass of wine and my dad is probably in a food coma somewhere.

I heard the footsteps of the notorious Izzie The Iceman coming closer... getting louder... as the sweat now profusely pouring from my head and armpits I closed my eyes knowing this was the end, then just as I was prepared to die I heard....

"Hey Freddie, everything's fine back here. I'm not gonna ruin my

suit bending down to open the god-damn crate!"

Alright!... Alright! Get up here we're gonna take off, sit the fuck down!"

Just then Joey and I looked at each other knowing we would live to see another day... maybe. The doors to the plane were already locked and the engines were now roaring, ready to roll down the runway into the heavens and back to Brooklyn we go.

Back To Brooklyn

We must have fallen asleep during the long flight back to New York because I don't remember anything after we took off. It must have been all the excitement and the thought of being killed made me sleepy …. yea, that's it. Meanwhile, my brother miraculously was still sleeping, either sleeping or dead but I didn't smell anything so my guess is on sleeping. As I very slowly put my hand over his mouth I gave him a nudge to wake up. One nudge… two nudges… finally I rolled him over like a beached whale and straddled him with my hands firmly over his mouth so he wouldn't scream and we wouldn't die.

We must have been in a hanger because I heard men talking and I needed to hear if they were going to come and take the crate with the salad. If they were, that meant we were going to die here and now, if they weren't we had a chance to get the hell out of here… with the salad!

"How much we gettin for that salad Sonny?"

"Izzie, I told you not to ask so many questions, just do your job and watch the plane."

"Freddie, you and Nickie take the guns and bring the car around. Leave the salad crate till we get back, Izzie you watch the plane."

Okay great, they're only taking the guns. *GUNS!* Where the hell were the guns? I kept telling myself....*BREATHE DEEP!*

Car doors slamming and they're gone, now we only have to get passed nut-so Izzie The Iceman and geez, I never asked why he was called the Iceman because well, I think it implied why.

As I motion to my brother to keep quiet I very slowly and quietly crawl out from under the tarp that was now nicknamed our tomb, to see where this lunatic was. Looked out this window and no Izzie... okay I'll look out the other window on the other side.... and then it happened...*SONOFABITCH!* When your foot hits head on into a large crate you know it and as I crashed to the floor of the plane holding my tongue and my foot I knew I would soon find out where the Iceman was. Sure enough, here he comes to investigate where that loud bang came from and here I was again... under our *tarp tomb!*

It took about five minutes which seemed like five hours for the Iceman to have a look around and leave. Meanwhile I couldn't help but think how stupid can he really be to not notice the bulges which were us under the tarp were not only noticeable but they moved! Talk about lucky for us and *stunade* for him!

Okay... so let's try this again. Peeking out the window I notice *Dumb-ass Iceman* is having a smoke away from the hanger, far away...as a matter of fact... he just kept on walking, farther and farther away. This was our chance and we are taking the salad with us... only to figure out how!

Quick as lightning Joey and I uncovered ourselves and the crate and as it turns out, it wasn't that big of a crate after all...

"Joey, look around for something to pry this open."

My plan was to take the salad out of the crate and run like hell with it back to Bobby Baccala's house. Easy right? Sure it was, if only I knew where the hell I was!

Here comes my brother with a huge spoon! Yep, you guessed it... a friggin Sunday gravy stirring pot spoon! Why would kitchen utensils be on a plane that doesn't have a kitchen? I'm kinda guessing these guys kill people with kitchen utensils instead of guns and knives... or maybe... *NO WAY!* Okay, now I'm gonna throw up!

No time to waste, I took the spoon from my brother and started to pry this million dollar crate open.

One... Two...Three...Four...Five... hey, we're kids... it took awhile.

BANG... IT'S OPEN! There is was grandma's priceless, town crumbling, earth shattering, worth dying for friggin Tortellini Salad and I have it. As I held this priceless sought after Tortellini Salad bowl in my hands I turned to my brother, as we both looked at each other I said... *RUN!*

I gave my brother the salad bowl to hold while I opened the plane's door and we both flew out of the plane with lightning speed. I looked frantically around for a getaway vehicle because that was the only way we were getting away!

"Joey, stay here while I look for a car!"

"You don't drive!"

"Now, I do! Stay here!"

Two minutes later I pull up in a black caddy, what I like to call the ultimate mobster car. I rolled down the window and yelled, *"Get In!"*

And wouldn't you know it, there's my brother sitting reading a magazine with the million dollar salad packed in dry ice, clueless as ever, out in the open where anyone on the planet can see him.

He should've had a bulls-eye on his back or a friggin sign that said shoot me.

So I yelled again…

"Hey, get in the car… now!"

"AND BRING THE SALAD!"

Oh my God, I swear this is all a very bad dream and I will soon be waking up like nut'n happened.

Now I know we didn't land in Kennedy or LaGuardia because there was a sign that said Teterboro New Jersey and this was not an airport everyone in the world goes to. Off to Brooklyn we go and as soon as we got on the New Jersey Turnpike Joey noticed a black car following us and of course I told him he was crazy…

"We're be'n followed."

"No we're not, your nuts. Just make sure that salad don't spill or anythin or I'll kill ya myself."

We merge onto I-80 then to I-95 and by now I was starting to get sweaty palms not to mention my heart was beating five thousand beats per minute because as I hated to admit it, I think we were being followed. As soon as we got to I-278 the last leg of our trip before Brooklyn I look in the rear view mirror and there is that black car, as always… one car behind all the damn way.

Eighty miles per hour and there it was… exit 32B the exit that will take us towards Metropolitan Avenue and in five minutes we will be home sweet home. As we arrive on Ainslie Street I slow down to a crawl purposely to see what this so called stalker/follower does.Still behind me I pull into the nearest parking space I could find because in Brooklyn, if you don't grab a space you don't get any…ever!

We sit… we wait… the car very slowly passes us… we turn our heads… *v e r y   s l o w l y!* Our eyes meet and it was him…*Izzie The Iceman!* He passed slowly, driving down the block and as he turned the corner we looked at each other simultaneously and let out the biggest and loudest scream…

"AHHHHHHHHHHH!"

"Get Out!… Get out of the friggin car and take that salad, now Joey!" I screamed with incredible panic racing across my face. I was moving at the speed of light while my insides were convulsing, my body temperature was rising and sweat was pouring from every pore of my body.

How the hell did he find us? Never mind that… how the hell did he follow us? That was the million dollar question at the moment. I left to get the car or rather "borrow" the car and it was only five or ten minutes. He left the area to smoke a cigarette and then… *"JOEY!"*

So here I am back in Brooklyn at Bobby Baccala's house with my clueless brother whose holding what we believe to be a tortellini salad that was stolen by three incredibly large hit-men and flown by private plane... the one we were stow-a ways on... back to New York... I hope someone else can understand this because... *"I CERTAINLY DON'T!"*

"Hey! What's all the banging about?"

"Oh My God, what the hell are you two doing back here?"

"Forget it Bobby, no time to explain while we're standing half on your stoop and half in the friggin vestibule, let's go upstairs....NOW!"

I pushed Joey in front of me to follow Bobby upstairs while I made sure the door was locked and took one last look to make double and triple sure that a mad man wasn't standing right behind that door waiting to kill us. I could just read the papers now, the headlines would say.... TWO BROOKLYN KIDS MURDERED BY THE MOB FOR A SALAD! Up the stairs we flew and right into Bobby's kitchen...

"Okay, does somebody wanna explain what you two are doin here, in my kitchen, holding a box with supposedly as you say, a salad inside?"

"Okay Bobby, you need to sit down for this one. I'll explain it one time and only one time.... Capisce?!"

We all sat down very slowly as if we were waiting for the end of the world and it may as well have been judging how my life was unfolding. I told Bobby the entire story and by the end of it he looked like he saw a ghost, eyes wide and jaw unhinged, he was in shock and disbelief all at the same time. Then he said it...

"Ah c'mon! Your full a shit! There is no way any mafioso hit-man is after two kids with a friggin tortellini salad!"

That was it, one of my best friends thought I was nuts. So I turned to my brother and turned to look back at Bobby and said...

"Okay wise ass, let's open the box and I'll prove to you that there's a salad in there. Do you think I missed my friends so much that I had my grandmother make a salad so I could hop a plane and bring it to your friggin doorstep! Do you?"

Now I was getting pissed off, not only was Bobby laughing at me but I have a salad sitting in a Tupperware in a box packed in dry ice that probably isn't cold anymore!

"Joey, open the box."

"Why me?"

"Because you're younger than we are and I said so!"

"You're not mom!"

"I'm not dad either but since they are like a million miles away and we have Izzie The Ice Pick or whatever the hell he's called

after us, I will have to do… now open the friggin box!"

"Would you two stop it, let's all open the box!"

One… Two… Three…it's open, now for the Tupperware to unveil the literally "to die for" salad. Believe it or not, it was still cold.

"There you have it!" Joey said pointing to the salad. *"It's just a salad, that smells incredibly good, let's have a taste."*

"NO! Screamed Joey. *"There may be a bomb in it, like in the movies, you bite into one and the whole kitchen goes up!"*

"Give me a fork, I'll taste it!" I said, not really caring at this point after all, how much worse can it get?

"OH MY GOD! It smells delicious, okay here goes the taste test. Oh hey guys, if I die all my worldly possessions go to my grandmother in Italy, she was really cool."

"Don't worry, we'll ship ya back in the tortellini box!" Said Bobby, while laughing his ass off.

"OUCH! I screamed. *"Are tortellini's suppose to be hard inside?"* As I'm holding my mouth and thinking I just lost a tooth from a tortellini. *"Holy shit, I'm bleeding! I think I chipped a friggin tooth!"*

Just then I see Bobby and my brother Joey rise at the same time from their chairs to look down at the bitten tortellini still on the fork that I threw down onto the table, Bobby and Joey both looked at me in horror, just then Bobby said...

" I think you got bigger problems than a tortellini salad."

The Zillion Dollar Rock

Now my life—up to this very day—has been rather simple. As a matter of fact, the only worries any of us had were basically maintaining straight A's in school and most importantly, wondering which one of our mothers were going to cook the best dinner on any given night. But here we were, my brother Joey and my best friend Bobby standing around his kitchen table with our eyes as wide as silver dollars and our jaws hitt'n the floor. We were paralyzed as we gazed in disbelief and horror at what we saw before us on the table.

There it was, the half bitten tortellini still semi-attached to the fork and sparkling little rocks—not just any rocks—*DIAMONDS!* We all looked at each other very slowly as if our eyes would fall out of our heads if we moved to fast. I was afraid to breathe and I didn't know if I could, then very slowly and just above a whisper I said, *"Are these what I think they are, Bobby?"* He looked at me with a horrified stare and said, *" They sure as shit are!"*

"Well then we better start opening a few of these. Whatddya think?" It was obvious I was gonna volunteer my brother to start opening some more, I mean, ya know, just in case something happens.

"Go ahead Joey, you open one."

"Why me!"

"Because I said so, now open it!"

And there they were, more tiny little sparkling stones. Once again we all were paralyzed, we couldn't breathe and then Bobby started...

"So let me get this straight, your grandmother—that sweet apron wearing, bun in hair old lady—is a jewel thief!"

"Fuck you Bobby!" I said as I wanted to jump over the table and knock my best friend to the floor.

"Oh yea!... Then what is the story genius!... You tell me! Because from where I'm standing this is how it looks to me...You all went to visit grand-mama in Italy who throws this big gigantor party every year for the entire mobster world. You meet family you never seen before, who all wear black and turns out some or all are hit-men and they steal—now get this, here's the good part—they steal A SALAD, which in turn the entire fucking town goes bat-shit crazy over...once again... here's the good part...A SALAD!"

I had nothing to say, I just looked at Bobby, looked at my brother and looked down at the diamonds and tortellini's and I knew what Bobby was gonna say, so I saved everyone the trouble and said it out loud myself.

"My grandmother is the Don!"

"No she's not," said Joey. *"That's grandma Pecorino and you're an idiot!"*

Just then my urge to strangle my brother was stronger than ever, I would have gladly given him over to Izzie…by the way where was the murdering pick-ax guy? Just as I finished thinking it a knock on the door and it wasn't a tap this was a bang kinda knock, only the kind a crazy, scary, ugly murderer can do. We froze once again as if to draw straws magically by the looks we were giv'n each other. Bobby slowly walked down the hall to the front door to look through the peep-hole, then we heard it….

"What the fuck Frankie, you don't know how'da call?"

What a relief it was just Frankie Fagioli.

"Heeey you're back!… How was your trip, boy that was a fast trip you weren't even gone two weeks. Good, I'll tell my ma you guys are back, she wants to call your ma."

"NOOOOOO!" We both screamed together. Just then Bobby grabbed Frankie and we all went back into the kitchen. There was

Frankie face to face with the diamond covered kitchen table.

"Holy fuckin cannoli! What the hell is this?...Hey before you guys get pinched my ma could use a nice necklace."

"No Frankie, don't touch anything!" I screamed as I pushed his hands away from the table. Just then Frankie had the exact same horrified look as we all did, he looked as if he realized he just crawled into the shit-pot and he was waist deep in shit.

Just then I said, *"Frankie, you better sit down for this one."* And I went on to explain this unbelievable story once again as it played over and over again in my head.

"Frankie, it all started when we landed..."

As I finished telling Frankie how this all came to be he didn't look very surprised at all and he said to Bobby and me that he had an idea, just as he got the word "idea" out of his mouth another bang on Bobby's door...

"Bobby," I said. *"Is that your mother?"*

"Naaa, she's out with Anna Maria, they shop till the moon comes up."

"Well, if it's not your mother, we got problems."

Joey ever so conveniently reminded me that Izzie The Iceman

should be showing up any moment now.

"Okay, everybody listen to me...HIDE!!!!!"

Joey and I hid in Bobby's mother's coat closet... yeah, I know...it was stuffy and hot in there. I felt like a sausage cooking in my mother's oven and it had this weird smell in between fish and moth balls...*Ewwww!*

Just then we heard Bobby answer the door...

"Hi Mrs. Mortadella, how are ya!"

"Oh... Hi Bobby...Oh my God look how big you're gett'n you must grow five inches every hour. Is your mother home?"

"Naaa, mom is out with my cousin Anna Maria, they went shopping and you know how that goes."

"Oh okay, here give her this. I made some of my cannoli with the chocolate chips for her to try. Tell her they didn't have the pistachio's at the store."

"Okay, thank you Mrs. Mortadella, I'll make sure she gets these."

At last, we could breathe as I opened the dead fish–moth ball smelling closet door. It was like a tornado of fresh oxygen stormed our lungs as I pushed my brother out into the room.

"Hey! We got cannoli! C'mon get in here!" shouted Bobby.

I didn't have to hear that twice.

So here we all were sitting around Bobby's kitchen table stuffing cannoli down our throats and acting like it was just another day when in fact we have a stolen tortellini salad that is not a real salad at all which had a ton of diamonds stuffed into the tortellini and a hit-man for the mob from Italy looking to make me the next can of Alpo... other than that... it was just a normal day.

"Oh man, I'm gonna need a bigger pant size if I keep eat'n like this," said Frankie patting an already bulging stomach. Then it happened...*BANG! BANG! BANG!* and it wasn't fireworks, it was the front door and I don't think it was Maria Mortadella again bringing more food. We all looked at each other because we all knew...especially me...at that moment there wasn't a friendly neighborly face on the other side of that door. He'd come back and I knew he would but this time I thought, did he bring others, were there guns...of course there were guns...the question was...how many goons were there and most importantly were they all behind the door or climbing up the fire-escape to take us by surprise. Just then, Frankie Fagioli had an idea...

The Plan

Frankie's idea was to first go to Scungilli's butcher shop on the avenue and Augie Scungilli would gladly give us some more dry ice to pack the salad in, since Augie and Vinny Baccala, Bobby's father play cards together every Friday night at the club. Bobby still won't tell me what kind of club it really is but anyways...

Bobby thought it was a great idea and that's exactly what we did. Off we go to Scungilli's with salad in hand for ice, Mr. Scungilli was always a real sweet guy, always smiling and laughing ready to tell a story or two to his customers with is Italian/English accent. A little English and little Italian and they all understood every word he said because our neighborhood at the time was mostly Italian and many of our friend's parents spoke the language very well, since they also came from Italy.

Anyways...

So there we were with a tortellini salad filled with a ton of diamonds packed in dry ice. The next move according to Frankie was to put the salad in one of his mother's shopping bags and cover it with old clothes that she gives away to charities. Then we all would go back to my house where my brother Joey would get in through the storm cellar in the backyard and open the front door for us so we can get our red Radio Flyer wagon and that's how we would transport the salad. Simple, right? What could possibly go wrong with this entire plan?

"Are you sure this is gonna work, Frankie?" says Bobby.

" Trust me, of course it will!"

"Yeah, and what are we gonna do with a salad in a friggin wagon? What we need is a car Frankie, a friggin car!"

"Listen guys!" I shouted, *"Let's leave the salad here in the bag covered with these clothes, no one's home and we can go look for a car we can borrow."*

"Borrow?" Frankie said.

"Frankie, we all know you know how to hot-wire a car, your sister taught you!"

" I heard that isn't all she went around teach'n the guys!" said my brother Joey as he busted out into laughter.

"J-O-E-Y!" we all shouted together. *"Not cool Joey...not cool."* I

said while pulling him to the front door.

So that's what we did. We left the salad in the bag with the clothes covering the cooler that the dry ice was in that held the zillion dollar salad while the four of us went to find a car to hot-wire to take us to *I-don't-know-where.* Keep in mind neither one of us has a driver's license so legally driving anywhere was out of the question, so was hot-wiring a car and come to think of it I was pretty sure nothing was legal about any of this.

"Bobby, why don't we use that sweet sports car your sister has, she's away at your aunt's in Jersey, isn't she?"

"Frankie, my mother and father would kill me, are you crazy?"

"Oh yeah, apart from Izzy the Ice-pick guy and his hit-men killing you?" he said. *"I'd take the chance of your mother and father killing you."*

So that's what we did. Balbina Baccala had a 1970 Pontiac Trans-Am, a hard muscled commando of a sports car with a terminal velocity of 103.2 mph in a bad-ass blue... and we stole it. *B-A-M!* just like that, Frankie Fagioli was the master if hot-wiring cars and in under three minutes we were off back to the house to get the Tortellini salad in the shopping bag.

"Joey, did you leave the front door open?" I asked calmly as panic swept through my entire body.

"I don't think so!"

"S-O-N-O-F-A-B-I-T-C-H!" I screamed in horror as everyone came running only to see no bag, no salad and the feeling of nausea in the pit of my stomach.

"Holy Shit!...What the fuck!" said Frankie in horror.

"Oh this is bad, very bad guys," said Bobby shaking his head.

Then we heard a lady's voice, an Italian lady's voice like a grandma voice coming from the upstairs bedrooms. It was like we were in a bad dream, and let's face it, I've been in this bad dream since the third of July, this was an ongoing nightmare for me...

"Helloooo... who come-a home-a?" she said as we slowly walked to the staircase. Then I saw her, it was my neighbor Mrs. Salami, Sarafina Salami who comes to check on the house since we left.

"Oh Mrs. Salami," I said trying not to show sweat and panic. *" How are you?"*

"Oh my-a, what-a you do home-a?"

Now, I had to think of something clever and believable at the same time.

"Uh... Joey got sick so ma told us to fly home to take him to the doctor... yeah, that's it...we have to go to the doctor."

"Oh, I-a see," she said, while nodding her head with half of the nods believing me and half being very confused. I think we all were confused.

"Say Mrs. Salami did you happen to see a bag...a shopping bag full of clothes right here when you came in?"

Now my heart was beating four-thousand beats per minute and I could feel the sweat beads dripping down the sides of my face. I was trying to keep composed while dying on the inside.

Then she replied...

"Oh the bag-a, I give-a to sister Catarina Caprese for the children."

"Your sister, Mrs. Salami?" I said very slowly and carefully.

"Oh Noooo," she said while do'n all those Italian gestures with her hands...

"Sister Catarina, from the orphanage."

I think at that moment I swallowed what felt like stones...no boulders inside my throat.

"Mrs. Salami, where is the orphanage, is it around here?"

I was making motions with my hands like the orphanage was right there in my friggin house!

"Oh Noooo...Sister Catarina take-a the bag-a to Italy, Rome-a

she take-a the bag-a."

Now I know...no...I'm sure I'm having a stroke! I feel my head turn all the way around to look at Frankie, Bobby and my brother and I'm pretty sure we all had the same expression of shock on our faces. My mouth was dry and I'm pretty sure my tongue was swollen, I could even feel twitching going on but what body parts exactly were twitching...I don't know.

So just in case you're just tuning in to the saga of my life and death, allow me to fill you in...

I get on my very first plane ride for the very first time to Italy to see grandparents I never met before...for the very first time. We get lost, my mother's extended family in Italy look like the entire cast from the movie *The Godfather.* My grandmother throws a party that Hollywood and royalty would be jealous of, a tortellini salad that she makes is the number one attraction...it gets stolen, the entire town goes nuts. My brother and I follow the stolen salad back to Brooklyn with the hit-men that stole it...find out the tortellini's are stuffed with diamonds...hit-men chasing us...stole a car...salad stolen again! I sure hope you got all that because I'm sure confused right about now.

Okay…back to Sister whats-her-name and the whereabouts of the friggin salad!

I turn back to Mrs. Salami and say…

"Mrs. Salami, do you know when the flight is leaving?"

"Oh yes…yes, night-a -time-a…tonight-a."

"Do you by any small chance know the flight number?"

I know I was really reaching here for answers I knew weren't happen'n, but hey…I asked anyways…and then it happened….

"Yes…yes, I-a remember very bad-a-number, 1-6-6-6 out of the President-a airport-a."

Okay so we have a flight to Italy leaving tonight from Kennedy with what we think is flight number 1666. I couldn't thank her fast enough as we ran out of the house jumped into the Trans-Am and back to Bobby's house to get a few things, devise a plan and get our asses to Kennedy International Airport to…yep you guessed it…become stow-a-ways on a commercial flight to Italy.

When In Rome...

Wiping the sweat from our faces, back at Bobby's house we had to come up with a plan and fast because we only had a few hours before it would be dark and we still had to drive to the airport and well, neither one of us had driver's licenses.

"Bobby, we should get cleaned up, like showers and stuff," Frankie suggested while wiping sweat and grime with Bobby's mother's *mopeen.*

"Yeah, that's a great idea," I said. *"Clean clothes and showers and off to the airport for Italy, we have plenty of time."*

Another knock on the door, ***BANG! BANG! BANG!*** Only this time we waited, silent and still...we waited.

BANG! BANG! BANG! ...

"Who the hell is it now!" said Bobby.

Bobby reluctantly goes to the door and that's when we all hear...

"Hey, I saw the Tranny outside are we all going for a ride?" It was Paulie Polenta our other partner in crime and this time he truly was going to be. While everyone was getting ready I sat and told Paulie everything from the beginning and again the look of shock and horror, no surprise there and Paulie was on-board with us, the gang was together and we were going to conquer the Mafia, in Italy....yeah, right!

We were ready, squeaky clean and it's a good thing we all were about the same size because we were all wearing Bobby's clothes and one last look once again at the city I love so much, my home Brooklyn New York. I thought this could be it, I may never return...we may never return...or I may return only in a pine box...nah...we're good.

"Everybody get in and hold on, Kennedy Airport here we come!"

"Frankie, are you sure you know how to get there?" I asked.

"Of course Frankie knows!" said Paulie. *"Don't you remember how we used to shoot fireworks off in the marshes there before we got caught!"*

"DRIVE!" said Bobby. *"Enough with the bullshit, we're burning daylight here!"*

What would normally be a forty-six minute drive with no traffic in ideal conditions now seemed like a nightmare at three-thirty in the afternoon on a weekday. We had to take I-278 East to the Grand Central Parkway for about five miles to I-678 South to Kennedy Airport and if you were born on another planet and don't know Kennedy Airport let me tell you there is no easy anything when trying to park or catch a plane, although in our case we were just hooking a ride overseas.

Frankie likes speed and so proceeds to drive like a lunatic on fire as we cut off three disco dudes in dago tees, they had so much friggin grease in their hair I'm surprised they didn't slide out of their car when they slammed on the brakes due to Frankie being an idiot. We all look over smile and wave and they return the favor with the famous one finger wave, New York style and that's all they had to do...

"Fuck you, asshole!" screams Frankie.

"Frankie, shut up!" I said. *"You're gonna get us killed!"*

Paulie starts to laugh and says, *"Yeah, you're worried about dying, I'll tell them to kill ya with kindness...he he he."*

"Paulie," Bobby said. *"That's an oxymoron."*

"You're all morons, now just drive the damn car!" Screamed my brother Joey. After that, there wasn't a word said till we got to the airport, then the fun began.

Parking at the airport is no joke and Frankie did not care at this point where to park the car. We choose the garage parking or extended parking, as we pull up to the machine we take the ticket, no problem, right?

"Hey Frankie, you got money on ya?" I asked out of curiosity.

"Nah, we'll sort it out when we get back, don't worry."

"I can't believe you," said Paulie. *"You're worried about paying a friggin parking ticket, like that's all you got to worry about."*

"Ya know, if I recall you're in the shit pot with us, so if we go down...so do you!" I said.

Alitalia Airlines was the obvious choice and now to find flight 1666. I walk up to the desk and ask the lady if there was a flight 1666 leaving tonight for Rome and sure enough, there was! That was about the only piece of luck I had since this nightmare began oh and not getting into a fatal car wreck on the expressway. Then I proceeded to ask if Catarina Caprese was listed on the flight, I told the lady at the check-in that it was my aunt and I missed her when the family said goodbye and that of course I would be heartbroken if I didn't get to say goodbye after-all she may never be back here again. She checked the passenger list for the flight and again a stroke of luck, she was on it.

She proceeded to tell us that the plane had already boarded and it was the last call and how sorry she was that I missed my beloved aunt but she couldn't let us on the plane. We were getting on that plane if we had to strap our asses to the wings…we had to come up with a plan and fast. As luck would have it Ms. Lady-Check-In gets called away by a guy in uniform, probably her pilot boyfriend and just at that moment we took advantage of the opportunity to become stow-a-ways to Italy.

Once on the plane we all proceeded to calmly walk down the aisle while our eyes surveyed every face and every bag in the cabin. After-all, how many nuns could be on a plane to Rome? It looked like a convention of the Immaculate Conception, they were everywhere! They wore black, they wore gray, they wore long habits and not so long habits, some had one cross around their neck while others had around their necks what looked like the cross Jesus carried to Golgatha and they all looked back at us and smiled, we were kids, we looked innocent. I kept waiting to get hit with a paddle for all my sins and right about now, they were many. Then I saw her, the window seat in the second to last row in this ginormous plane, Sister Catarina Caprese and the shopping bag with my tortellini salad.

The entire eight hours and twenty minutes of flying time the four of us spent playing musical seats in the back of the plane and we occupied the bathroom so much I was starting to feel at home in there and trust me when I say, turbulence is not fun inside a bathroom on a plane. We did manage to eat a nice meal and hang-out in the lounge area of the gigantic plane while one of us always kept eyes on Sister Caprese and the bag. Finally the announcement for trays up and seat belts on for the final decent to Rome. I kept having the feeling of deja-vu and rightly so at these point I should have been getting frequent flyer miles.

We finally landed, all eyes on the nun and the bag.

"Follow that nun!" I said while pointing to this tiny four-foot-eleven petite woman carrying a shopping bag she easily could have fit in. We were like her shadow, only she had four shadows following her every move. I was suspecting she was going to grab a cab to take her to who-knows-where, just then my brother Joey nudges me with a very confused check-this-out look on his face. Ms. "Shopping Bag Nun" wasn't heading to the cab stands at all she was getting on another plane! Then silently Paulie and I said it together... *"Fuck!"* Which now meant, how the hell are we gonna pull this off. This wasn't your average commercial airline, she was taking an Italian puddle-jumper called Gabagool Airlines and they only go two places, Capri and Sicily and what's in Sicily... Scarola!

"I gotta pee." said Joey.

"Yeah, that's a good idea, we could all use some water on our faces." Frankie agreed with my brother and we all agreed we needed to freshen up.

Bobby stayed within viewing distance of Sister Caprese while we all took turns peeing and freshening up. The fight #666 was leaving in two hours so we had enough time to watch her and maybe get something to eat and drink.

All cleaned up and ready to rock-n-roll another nine hundred hours we find this little place called *Chooch's* to grab a bite.

"Hey Bobby, this menu is in Italian."

"Yeah, so? We're in Italy, what language did you expect it to be in, Russian?" said Bobby.

"Okay smart ass, then which one of us knows how to read Italian?"

"I do." I said. *" I know a little from my mother."*

"Okay, then what's this?" asked Paulie.

"That right there?" I had to ask because I wasn't sure if this was a joke or my friend just being incredibly stupid. *"That's Ravioli you idiot, you're in the right place you chooch!"*

Our food consisted of all our favorites, for starters a simple mixed salad with genuine olive oil, vinegar and salt and pepper, then pasta al pomodoro…that's fresh tomatoes, olive oil and basil, some bruschetta doused in olive oil, langoustines sauteed with olive oil, garlic, onion and white wine and everyone's favorite individual pizza's topped with prosciutto. We ate it all and we were stuffed and just in time to stow-away on another flight. Lucky for us, Sister Caprese was dining in the same establishment, no coincidence there! We finished...she finished and back to being her shadow to the gate, it was all going so well until she stopped in mid-stride and turned around in a flash, looked at all of us and said...

"Excuse me young ones but it seems to me you have been up my habit since we left New York. Now either you are homeless and going to the orphanage to get adopted, which I highly doubt or you're all planning on robbing me which I can tell you right now that would be a huge waste of your time because all I have is this bag full of old donated clothes and last but not least, you all want an education on becoming part of a religious order in Italy, now which one will it be?"

There was complete silence as we froze in our places, we were each waiting for the other to start to speak and well since this was my nightmare unfolding, I was the one whose tongue the cat didn't get. *"No! Sister Caprese you got it all wrong...."*

I started to explain the story from the part when Mrs. Salami the Italian neighbor/house-watcher gave my bag by mistake to her and I went on to explain my mother's favorite dish is at the bottom of the bag, with fingers and toes crossed that she bought it. Surprisingly enough at that moment her attitude changed from beating the living shit out of all of us to feeling sorry for kids so far from home.

"Oh you poor children, you came all this way just so you could bring back your mother's favorite dish, when you could have just asked me for it at the airport in New York....Listen up buster, I was born in the day but not yesterday and if you think for one minute I'm fooled by your half ass story, you got another thing coming, my friend. Remember...I'm from Brooklyn and that was before I became a nun! Now, come over here and sit, we have an hour before I board the next plane and you are all gonna tell me the truth...what's in the bag!

I thought...no, we all thought this just can't get any worse but it already was heading in that direction. So, for the sake of not burning in hell we all sat calmly and I started telling her my saga of a nightmare from the very beginning....again. When I was done there was a moment of awkward silence as she looked at each one of us with her blue eyes burning holes through the back of our heads, like she was reading our minds or like God was telling her if I was lying or not; then she spoke.

"Okay, listen to me and listen very carefully, I know people...important people, but I want in on the money!"

"What money?" I said. *" We have hit-men after us and do you*

think I fuck'n know where to take these diamond filled tortellini's, who do you think I am lady…Sonny Corleone?"

"Watch your mouth!" she said, as her five fingers flew across my face! *"Follow me and be quiet!"*

She didn't have to say that twice, we couldn't believe what was unfolding before our eyes. I kept thinking, not only do I suspect my grandmother is the head of a Mafia family now we met a rogue nun who wants to get in on the game in the world of organized crime, who thinks she's Ma Barker! I'm really starting to get a migraine and just then Frankie said in a low whisper…

"Hey, maybe she was planted and she's part of your grandmother's crew and she really isn't a nun, it's just a disguise."

Oh my God! I think I'm having a stroke!

Sicily

At the boarding gate of Gabagool Airlines, Ma Barker in the nun outfit pawned us off as orphans going to the orphanage, trust me we didn't look like orphans. All I kept thinking about was that once in Sicily we can lose the penguin-in-drag and get to Scarola back to my grandmother's house and get some answers to a zillion questions I had, if we didn't get killed first. Oh yeah, and what about my parents, did they still remember they had children or were they part of this crime fest, maybe my mother's nickname is Sophia The Strangler.

Once we landed, Lizzy Borden had a car waiting for her and the driver did not look like a priest, more like Dr. Jekyll and Mr. Hyde posing as a priest, like I'll-stab-you-in-the-back kind of guy with a patch over one eye. Nothing good can come from this.

We hesitantly got into the car, everyone followed my lead like I knew what I was doin, what a joke. I knew I was having a stork, I knew I was about the shit my pants and I definitely knew I have no idea where we were going. I knew we landed in Palermo because well...the signs were everywhere! To get to Scarola we would have to drive west and a bit south, you know just follow the sea. At least this car was air conditioned and comfortable not like the oven-baked-fish-smelling cab we took from the airport on the first hell flight here. Just when we were starting to enjoy the scenery she spoke, breaking the heavenly silence that was to be our last car ride ever.

"Hey kid, you wanna drink?"

We all looked at each other to figure out which one of us she was asking in her gangster I'm-gonna-cut-your-throat kind of way. Bobby turned to her with a death stare and said...

Tell us the truth, Sister-whoever-you-are...who the fuck are you?"

"They'll be enough time for answers to all your questions, little smart-ass, right now shut the fuck up and enjoy the ride."

Okay, at this very moment we all knew this bitch wasn't a nun and the only thing she had "nun of" was class and neither did we but we were on a mission not to get killed, she on the other hand was on a mission to do the killing. After a very long and silent ride along the coast we arrive in the city of Trapani a western city in Sicily known for it's wine and olives and other artifacts but I was mostly interested in the wine at this point. We pull up to this long...long...long driveway like in those fancy pictures of English countryside estates where you can't see the castle on the other side of the fifty thousand acres, yeah that kind. Then I see it, we all see it...*Benvenuto Alla Cantina Bolognese*...Welcome To Bolognese

Winery! Owned by none other than the infamous Bolognese Crime Family...we were dead. The drive, "Mr. Hyde" pulls up the the very large door and we all just sat while I held onto the bag with the diamond filled tortellini salad with a death grip, which seemed appropriate given the state of events.

"Stay put and don't try to run, you won't make it. I'll be back in a minute," she said while pointing to all of us. After the huge dungeon door closed behind her, our silence was broken...

I turned to Frankie with concern and said, *"Frankie, you look sick, you can't die now and there's no doctors around here."*

"Except Dr. Jekyll in the driver's seat," said Paulie.

" Ha... yeah and you don't want him cuttin into you, ha...ha!" said my brother who was amused by this entire situation. He thought he was in a movie and you know, after a while I was hoping it was a movie by Martin Scorsese, you know....a movie about Williamsburg and the Mafia and we were all actors! Sorry Joey, this is no movie and the only actors here are all the creepy people around us, only they're not acting!

The front door opens and here comes two servants, one looked like a butler and the other wore those black gown type of dress with her flaming red hair pinned neatly in a bun.

"So these two are our killers?"

"No, Bobby I think they are just here to escort us inside," I said.

"Aw, c'mon...we could take these two walking statues!"

"Paulie," I sneered, *"shut your mouth, before we really all get killed!"*

Just then the butler opened the car door...

"Out of the car and please follow me."

"Oh shit, they speak English and very well I might add," said Frankie snickering.

We followed Heckyll and Jekyll into the house. This place was huge, marble everywhere and a staircase that wrapped around from on side to the other. I kept thinking if anyone fell from that we would splatter like a fly under a fat man's shoe.

Bobby whispered, *"I bet we're goin to the dungeon."*

"Shhh, be quiet," I said.

"I could fly down that banister!" said Frankie.

"Shhhhhhh...just follow the bitch!" whispered Paulie.

Just as we suspected, we climbed about fifty million stairs up to the second floor where we were lead into a huge room with a huge T.V. and couches in a circle. Just then the butler speaks again...

"You get cleaned for dinner, new clothes, go ahead."

Well this wasn't so bad I thought but we'll have to do this with someone always holding on to the bag and whatever happened to Sister-cut-your-throat I wondered, where the hell did she disappear to? Who cares, I was getting into a much needed shower.

All cleaned and sitting waiting for Heckyll and Jekyll to fetch us to what we assumed would be our death or torture… or both. They came and took us to the dining area with a table you could fit my entire block in Brooklyn at and before our very eyes was an Italian feast fit for a king or in this case a *Don!* At first we all sat at one end of the ginormous table and it looked friggin stupid. I told everyone to spread out so we don't look like friggin deer caught in headlights or lambs to the slaughter. Look casual and relaxed I told them after all the food looked amazing. Then it happened…

A larger than life figure of a man accompanied by two gigantic muscular goons walk into the room, we all froze in our seats. I was so stiff I could feel the blood running through my veins, I could feel the beads of sweat pouring down Bobby's face that's how frozen with fear we all were. It was him, Don Vito Bolognese himself.

We were surely going to eat our last meal.

La Famiglia Bolognese

The Bolognese crime family was a very powerful family in Sicily. Vito's father, Baldassario Bolognese was the most feared Don in any crime family history. Legend has it, he treated women like queens and men of the family like royalty and his rivals and competition... well I heard there's really no one alive to tell that part of the story. When he died three years ago from a long illness...yeah, right... his young son Vito took over. I can clearly see where Vito gets his looks from. This was no gavone overweight guy who sits in front of the neighborhood pork store playing cards, Vito Bolognese was tall, muscular, well-dressed... probably a gazillion dollars in suits, dark hair kinda shaggy but short, piercing blue eyes and a wad of a mustache and get this...he had a woman every where he went. My first thought a guy this popular and good looking, why not married?

His mother Audenzia, which means fearless, looked the part. She looked a super model-celebrity-celestial being type. I've never seen anything like it. She had to be older than dirt is what I thought but hey anyone over twenty to us was older than dirt at the time. She had long hair and wore a beautiful gown, all this for dinner! Heckyll and Jekyll were there too, as a matter of fact it was Mr.

Heckyll the butler who rang the dinner bell and the servants started to serve, all of us.

There was an eery silence during dinner. We dined on fresh baked breads, various fish and vegetables and a ton of homemade pasta, we even had some wine and although we were all thinking how we would love to raid the liquor cabinet or the wine cellar, we settled for what was poured for us and it was yummy. Once the table was cleared Vito spoke and we all listened...

" I'd like to start by saying, you are not here as my enemies but my guests and that you will not be harmed."

Then he looked straight at me...

"I know who you are, what you are carrying and all of your travels."

Just then we all looked at each other in shock and Frankie blurted out, *"We didn't do anythin, honest. We had this crazy bat-shit nun who wasn't a nun and took us here and..."*

Just then she walked into the dining room like a tornado ripping through the flatlands, like fire and ice, it was her....

"You mean me, kiddies?" It was her, Sister-bleed-to-death...The-Grim-Reaper-of-the-mob! It was her but it wasn't her. No habit, well that didn't fool us anyway, high heels, short dress, long hair and she was actually pretty...holy shit!

"Let me introduce to you my sister, Andriana Bolognese, you know her as Sister Caprese...yes?"

I felt my delicious dinner start to make it's way up to my throat and I struggled to not puke all over their forty zillion dollar dining room set. Bobby, Frankie, Paulie and my brother looked pale and a little blue around the gills. We slowly acknowledged what he said by shaking our heads in agreement and not a sound was heard as he continued....

"I know you have the diamonds," he started to say. Just then I realized the shopping bag was gone. We were supposed to watch it, each one of us, we came all this way, this can't be happening. I will not be a martyr for my crazy-ass family, I need to go home...we all need to go home. As our eyes gazed down to the floor hoping we would spot the bag then he started to speak again...

"Looking for this?" he said while holding a medium sized pouch.

"Nah," Bobby said. *"We had a shopping bag of old clothes."*

"Yeah...that's it," We all agreed looking relieved.

"No, that's not it," said Sister-Mary-Magdalene or whatever her name was.

"This is what you're looking for," she said as she emptied the pouch on the table and out comes a zillion diamonds!

They looked like stars, pretty little stars glistening in the night sky like a pretty peaceful dream. But only this wasn't a dream, they weren't stars and I wasn't star gazing into the friggin sky. Just then Frankie stands up and protests...

"I swear, we didn't know they were in the salad...honest!"

"Calm down," said Vito. *"I'll tell you what I know and then we make a deal. These belong to Antonietta Pecorino, you know her as your nonna, we know her as the head of the Pecorino crime family of Scarola."*

Oh my God! I just about fell off my chair! Frankie, Bobby, Paulie and my brother all looked at me like I had TB or the black plague, I went from being in shock to being really pissed off, I looked back at them and shouted...

"Whaaaat!... You all think I'm involved!... Are you all fuckin crazy...do I look like a fuckin hit-man?"

"Man...and to think I dumped my sister's Trans-Am for this shit!" Bobby said.

"Shut-up Bobby!" I shouted. *"What do you need us to do?"* I said to Vito, standing tall looking at him dead in the eyes. *"I'll do it, I want this bullshit to be over with."*

It seemed as though we were in that dining room all night long, what was only about three hours seemed like a hundred.

Vito went on to tell us the second half of my nightmare, it turns out Izzie-The-Iceman, Freddie-The-Fish, Sonny-The-Sausage and Nickie-No-Thumbs my so-called cut-me-up-in-little-pieces, I'll-fit-you-with-cement-boots cousins from another time were really soldiers for the Bolognese crime family and it turns out my brother and I botched their plan when we became stow-aways on their private-ass plane to New York. Now, Izzie-The-Iceman and all his goons were after us to stuff us into tortellini's and I don't think we'd taste very good.

"So now," Vito said. *"You go back to your nonna and you tell her if she wants her diamonds back, we make a deal. I want to expand my winery and she has the land, tell her it's business. You all leave in the morning. If you refuse, you don't go home... you don't go anywhere ever again, so for now, stay...mangia bene!"*

And just like that he left. Where he went who the hell knows. All I kept thinking was first there's no way in hell I'm leaving here without those rocks and second... and most importantly... I want that kind of power! Not to mention the cool house on the hilltops.

"So get the fuck outa here, your grandmotha turns out to be the butcher of Scarola!" said Bobby.

"So what does that make you, third in line to the Capone and

Luciano fortune?" laughed Frankie.

"This is bullshit!" said Bobby. *"This shit ain't real, it's probably a movie and this is Martin Scorsese's summer house!"*

"C'mon, this is serious," Paulie said. *"Do you realize all the shit we've been through?"*

"Does that mean you gotta kiss grandma's ring?" laughed my brother uncontrollably, like it was a game.

"Hey listen shit-head," I said to Joey. *"If it wasn't for you hiding on that fuckin plane saving a salad all this would've never happened."*

"So then why did the entire town go fuckin nuts when grandma realized the salad was missing?" asked Joey.

"Yeah, that's a great question," said Frankie. *"Oh No!... Holy shit! Do you know what that could mean...the entire town is her friggin crew!"*

"NO WAY!" We all said simultaneously.

"Listen up!" I said. *"I am not leaving here without those friggin rocks, this is what we're gonna do. In a few hours, I'm gonna go downstairs and search for them, they can't be far. Frankie, you search up here on the other side of the staircase and Bobby you take the other side. Paulie and Joey, you come with me. We have a lot of ground to cover...we find them... we get the fuck outta*

here!"

"Even in their bedrooms?" asked Frankie.

"YES!"

"What if they hear us?"

"Then you'll just have to...BE QUIET!"

"Okay, everybody synchronize they're watches, we'll meet back here in one-hour, capisci?"

Very quietly like Mafia mice, Paulie, Joey and myself tiptoed down the extremely long staircase to the first floor. I didn't think they would be stupid enough to hide the pouch filled with diamonds where anyone could take it, but we had to try. We searched the dining room first because well... that was the last place we all were. It was perfectly clean no trace left behind that anyone had dinner there a few hours ago but then what do you expect from people who make it their living at not leaving a crumb, leg, arm or torso behind.

"Paulie, you search the kitchen and take Joey with you and be friggin careful!"

Just as they entered the ginormous kitchen the door hits my brother square in the face...*BANG!*

"SONOFABITCH!" screams Joey, as he falls backwards onto the floor hitting the dinning room chair.

"Joey, I'm tell'n ya if they we have to sacrifice someone tonight, it's gonna be you, now shut the fuck up!"

I open the door to the kitchen and what do we see but Paulie standing there with the refrigerator door wide ass open looking to munch!

"Are you both kidding me!" I screamed in a loud whisper. *"We're all gonna get fitted for cement boots, now start looking."*

When we finally put our heads to it, we covered every inch of the lower level and no pouch. Just as we start to walk into the marble covered foyer with fifty-thousand statues, here comes Bobby and Frankie from upstairs.

"No dice, nothin upstairs except snoring blood-sucking Italians that are dreaming of killing us and your entire family," said Bobby.

"Well, we still have the other side of this museum to check out, let's go," Frankie said.

Just as I reached to turn off the light in the dining area I stopped and had an idea. Just one more look a voice in my head told me… just one more look because it has to be in here. After-all, where would you hide the most valuable shit you have? Obviously not in the most common places, it would be hidden in plain sight. My eyes glanced around the room as I stood silent and still in the doorway. Then it hit me! I walked like I was on a mission, which I was, straight to the buffet server and sitting a top this very expensive Italian looking piece of furniture was a huge sterling silver platter with a big dome cover, you know the kind you see in horror movies that often had heads underneath them...yeah...that kind. As I approached the buffet I could sense the gang was standing in the doorway once they noticed I hadn't followed them. I turned very slowly to them and Frankie said...

"What the fuck are you doin!"

I smiled and put one finger up to my mouth... *"Shhhhhhh!"*

I turned back to stare at this sterling silver dome and I closed my eyes for a moment and I thought if ever there was a time for a miracle, now would be it...then I lifted the dome.

My brain was screaming and cheering all at the same time, *"Ahhhhhhhhh!"* There it was, the beautiful pouch filled with those tiny twinkling starry-like diamonds and as fast as we could all blink, we were outta there, headed to Scarola.

"Ice Eyes"

Most kids growing up have grandmothers that bake cookies, breads, pies and love to cook. My friends have these grandmothers, Bobby's grandmother makes homemade pizza to-die-for, Frankie's grandmother makes the best gnocchi around and Paulie's grandmother and grandfather have a bitchin garden in the yard, a place we love to go and pick our own tomatoes in the summertime. I especially love her pesto sauce from garden fresh basil over her homemade pasta. Don't get me wrong, my mother is one of the best Italian cooks around and between the four of us, I can assure anyone we would never ever go hungry and that goes for anyone who came to visit.

But these days the images are a bit fuzzy in my head, I couldn't get the image of my grandmother sitting at the head of this enormously long table with the rest of the gun-wielding crazies I now know to be my family, which includes my mother and father a.k.a. Bonnie and Clyde, and two goons standing behind grandma's chair on each side with Tommy-guns, fedoras and pin striped suits. I mean, seriously…who has this kind of fucked-up family?….apparently I did.

Usually from Trapani to Scarola which was part of San Vito Lo Capo on the gulf of Castellamare took about twenty-four minutes by car along the coast, we didn't have a car and it was the middle of the night. We had the diamonds, we made sure of that and we started running as far away from the Bolognese estate/wineries as fast as we could and the running soon became a snails-pace walking... hey, kids get out of breath too!

San Vito Lo Capo (*pronounced, San Vitu*) in Sicily is part of the province of Trapani and is beautiful. Known for it's beautiful mountains, beaches and olive groves... oh and it's numerous caves at the base of several mountains... yeah, and get this... one cave in particular is called *Caverna della Capra Guasto* which I found out means, "Cave of the Dead Goat" which was named by explorers who probably never got out, how poignantly put.

Anyways...

Scarola lies smack in the middle of San Vito Lo Capo, hence the mountains and the sea...the wine and the fish. Yeah, I know it's known for the olives but I guess when the dark side moved in they built wineries.

It took us what seemed like an eternity with aching feet to arrive in Scarola, when we did it was early afternoon and the Fountain was flowing with wine and believe it or not the friggin party was still going strong. I know I haven't been gone long but what-the-fuck, who throws parties that last for days... Italians, that's who.

When we entered the town the five of us looked like Wyatt Earp and the gang ready to fight at the O.K. Corral and as we walked from my perspective it seemed like the entire town knew exactly who we were, like they were all waiting for us, either to walk in alive or carried in, in coffins, but either way they were waiting.

We were dirty, tired and pissed off. No one more than me wanted this all to end and today was the day I was going to get answers, the answers I sought from the very beginning of this insane nightmare. It's amazing how fast you grow up when you are tested in a life and death situation and on this day, we all grew up pretty damn fast.

"Wow, this is your grandmotha's town?" said Paulie

"Yeah, she lives over there," I said pointing to her home.

"Holy crap she's got an ocean view!" stated Frankie with eyes as wide as silver dollars.

"I would live here forever!" said Bobby.

"I'll never live here," I said. *"I'm goin home to Brooklyn when this is over."*

Just then I see the other half of the *Five Points Gang,* my mother with arms open wide and a huge smile on her face. She acted like I went to the corner store for milk and bread, not the reaction of a mother whose kids were gone a few days and not to mention not being surprised seeing Bobby, Paulie and Frankie in tow.

"Oh my gawd, look who it is! Oh we all missed you so much, we were worried!"

"Really!" I sternly said with a death look in my eyes as I brushed past her into the house, while saying...

"Oh by the way ma, you know my friends from Brooklyn, right?"

We walked into the house like we owned it. We passed all of them, Robbie Ravioli, Sammy Sirloin, Charlie Cioppino, Frankie Braciole, Nickie-No-Thumbs, Freddie-The-Fish, Sonny-The-Sausage and yours truly, the madman himself... Izzie-The-Iceman. Everyone was there, outside, inside and all around the grounds, eating, drinking, smoking and partying. Food was everywhere like we never left, only when we left the town was in mass chaos looking for the stupid salad, maybe they all knew... maybe they didn't but I was going to get answers.

There was my grandmother sitting at the head of this long-ass dining room table and my grandfather sitting next to her, both surrounded by cousins, a.k.a. hit-men wearing black vests that matched their black trousers that went with their black jackets.

Bobby, Paulie, Frankie and my brother take a seat at the table, not me... I approach my grandmother with the pouch. I'm on a mission and very pissed off, I place the pouch on the table with my hand on it at all times. Then I speak...

"Talk, grandma, or should I call you Ice-Eyes?"

You see, I learned in my travels on the dark-side that mafioso hit-men like to give each other nicknames and they all usually have meanings, like Nicky-No-Thumbs got his thumbs chopped off by a rival hit-man and he wore gloves with fake thumbs in the them. Only the real bad-ass mobsters got nicknames, they gave my grandmother the name "Ice-Eyes" because of her piercing blue eyes and word has it, she was a ruthless killer at one time…yeah right, like I wouldn't put it past any of these so called family members to fit me and my friends with cement shoes at any given time.

"What do you want to know, my child?" she said in a very eerily calm manner.

"Well, let's see," I said. *"It's a long Fourth of July weekend… I leave Brooklyn and the party of the friggin year to get on a plane to a place I've never been…to see family I didn't know I had… only to find out that it's a fuckin carnival side-show from the get-go!… And…to put the cherry on the fuckin cake…*

"You watcha your mouth!" yelled Sonny…the fuckin sausage man.

"You shut the fuck up!" I said. *"Allow me to continue the nightmare…where was I…oh yes…to put the cherry on the fuckin cake I find out my grandparents are the most powerful organized crime family on this side of Sicily! Not to mention the fact I got my*

very best friends involved and we traveled back and forth across the ocean as stow-a-ways, met your crime family rivals...and...this is the best part... chased after a fuckin tortellini salad that really wasn't a real salad after-all. So...we are tired, hungry, dirty and I want answers...NOW!"

The last part of my rant was so loud the entire room and not to mention the house went silent. You couldn't hear a fuckin pin drop or in this case, bullet.

"Yes, I know," she said.

I swear, she was so calm with this half-ass smile across her face, no one in the world would think this sweet looking Italian grandma would be Ma Barker the ruthless killer!

"We made a deal."

"WHO...made a deal?" I asked.

Then he walked into the room, none other than Mr. Ladies Man...Vito Bolognese. I swear, I really was starting to know what it felt like to overdose on drugs. The five of us were sitting in a huge house filled with villainous whack-jobs and we were the ones waiting to be whacked!

"Your grandmother and I made a lucrative business arrangement. I get the land for the wineries and she gets the diamonds and everyone is happy. It's business kid."

Just then Bobby whispered to me...

"Is that like... keep your friends close and your enemies closer kinda shit?"

I was just wondering which side of the close-knit fence we were on.

"You brave-a children. I'm proud of all of you. In a few days we'll make like none of this happened...yes?" said my grandfather as he stood up with a wine glass.

"Let's drink to happy endings and la famiglia!"

Everyone clapped and nodded in agreement with Vito, my grandparents and the rest of the organized crime world that was before me. The celebrations continued as if nothing happened and we all left for New York the following day on Vito Bolognese's private jet.

Somewhere on the earth below us it was daytime and people were going about their normal lives, but for us it was the middle of the night. The cabin of the plane was dark except for tiny dimly lit lights above the windows. My mom and dad were having a drink up front by the bar area, Paulie, Frankie and Joey were out cold and Bobby and I had our eyes open staring into the abyss...until Bobby looked over at me and said...

"So are we really gonna make like none of this every happened?"

" I don't know Bobby, I don't know what we're gonna do. I know

we will never forget this and we'll never be the same."

"Yeah, I know. I think we should forget this ever happened and just go about our lives like it didn't," said Bobby before nodding off to sleep.

I turned to look out into the great endless wonderland of darkness that was all around us and before I gave in to the tranquility of slumber, I uttered just two words...

"Yeah...right."

Epilogue

Many years have come and gone since that chaotic Fourth of July in Sicily. Grandma and grandpa Pecorino are gone, some say grandpa was fitted for cement shoes and some say he joined Jimmy Hoffa, all in all, the seventies were a wild time for organized crime. Grandma died at one-hundred years with all of her loyal mobsters by her side, family too. I was there and so was Bobby, Paulie, Frankie and Joey of course. In fact, we all became quite close with grandma after that July, we would all call her often and she would send care packages to all of us filled with homemade pastas, wine, bread and of course wads of money for my father for his business, I never did quite know what his business was, he always did a "little of this and a little of that."

We all grew up since then.

My brother Joey now thirty-eight, became a New York City decorated detective. He lives in a four bedroom apartment over looking Central Park, he never married but dates a lot. He always had a beautiful woman on his arm. I'm proud of my brother.

Francesca (Frankie) Fagioli married a big time trader in the stock market, she became a high profile fashion designer with her own design label *Madre Tortellini*, it kinda sticks with ya! She's always traveling to and from New York and Milan showcasing her shoes, purses and clothes and of course I'm her biggest customer.

After getting her law degree, Paulina (Paulie) Polenta became the Chief Judge in New York's Court of Appeals. She married a chef who owns a little upscale Italian bistro called San Vitu and we all meet there for lunch and dinner whenever we get the chance, which is pretty regular.

My dearest friend of all, Barbara (Bobby) Baccala, always a thinker and fearless. She became a decorated F.B.I. agent in the Behavioral Analysis Unit. Never married, I guess because her job takes her everywhere. She still calls Williamsburg her home and when all the new high-rise condos went up, she purchased an entire building and lives in the penthouse where she has a roof-top garden and patio that she enjoys.

Last but not least…me.

I went on to take business education courses and studied wine making, the legitimate way. I married that Italian Sam Elliot look-alike mobster, Vito Bolognese, after-all he was only twelve years older than me back then. He was like fine wine that always gets better with age. Together, we run the "business" and the wineries in Sicily. My parents still live in Brooklyn and come to visit quite often any time they wish. My three sons are all in the "family business" and we have quite a few wineries all over Italy, Sicily and Greece and sell all over the world.

And the five of us always made sure no matter where we are in our lives we always get together on the Fourth of July for at least a week or more. Usually it is held here in Scarola, at my home over looking the Gulf of Castellamare, sipping wine and laughing and remembering those four days many years ago.

I'm Theodora (Teddy) Castellamare and you can bet your ass we definitely never forgot the year we chased after the Tortellini's.

THE END

Made in the USA
San Bernardino, CA
23 July 2019